MR. PROPHET

LOST AND FOUND

TITLES AVAILABLE IN BUZZ BOOKS

First published 1990 by Buzz Books,
an imprint of the Octopus Publishing Group,
Michelin House, 81 Fulham Road, London, SW3 6RB.

LONDON MELBOURNE AUCKLAND

Barney © 1989 Barney Entertainments Ltd

Text and Illustrations © 1990 Methuen Children's Books
Story by Stanley Bates
Illustrations by Edgar Hodges
From an original idea by Shirley-Anne Lewis
Licensed by Link Licensing Ltd
All rights reserved

ISBN 1 85591 021 7

Printed and bound in the UK by BPCC Paulton Books Ltd.

Barney's New Hair-Do

Story by Stanley Bates

Illustrated by Edgar Hodges

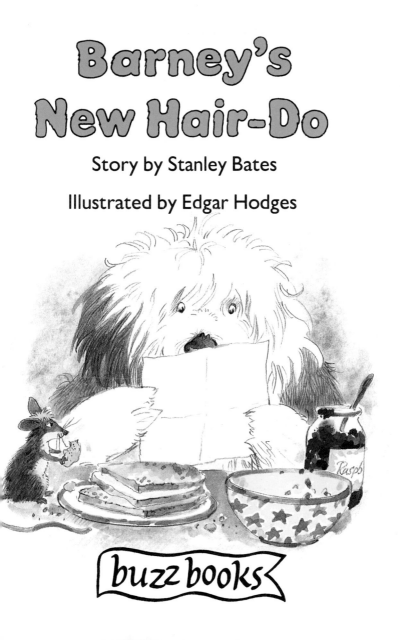

buzz books

Barney and Roger were having breakfast when they heard the postman. Roger dashed to see what had arrived.

"It's for you, Barney," he shouted. "A letter, and it's marked Urgent."

Barney tore open the envelope, read the letter and gasped.

"Who's it from?" asked Roger, who didn't like to be left out of things.

"From the television studios," said Barney. "A magazine wants to do a feature on me. They're sending a photographer over to see me this morning."

"How exciting," said Roger. He felt rather envious. He looked at Barney, then he looked again.

7

"Barney, I hope you don't mind me saying this, but I think we'll have to do something about you."

"What do you mean Roger, do something about me?"

"It's . . . just, well . . . you look a bit informal."

"What's wrong with that?" said Barney and he sauntered over to the mirror. "Oh!" he said. "I look dreadful. What shall I do?"

"Let's get Cornelia to come round. She'll
help you make the best of yourself."

When Cornelia arrived, she took one look
at Barney and said,

"A new hair-do, that's what you need.
First we'll wash it, then we'll style it. Where
do you keep the shampoo?"

"In the cupboard over there," said Barney.

"Roger, fetch a brush and comb please.
Barney, you go and stand in the bath."

"Do I have to?" grumbled Barney. "I
hate having baths."

9

"Do you want to look good for the photographer or don't you?" snapped Cornelia.

Roger filled the bath and Cornelia started to shampoo Barney. Soon he was covered in bubbles, and so were Cornelia and Roger, and so was most of the bathroom.

"What kind of shampoo is this?" asked Barney. "It's got a funny smell."

10

Cornelia looked at the bottle. "Oh dear," she whispered to Roger. "This isn't shampoo at all. It's for cleaning carpets."

"What did you say?" said Barney through the bubbles.

"I said 'you'll be the smartest!'" said Cornelia quickly, rinsing off the foam.

She gave Barney a quick rub with the towel and then she and Roger began to comb out his coat.

"Ow!" shrieked Barney, "that hurts."

"Sorry," said Roger, "but we've got to hurry. The photographer will be here soon."

"Come into the kitchen, Barney," said Cornelia. "We need more space."

"Now, watch carefully, Roger," said Cornelia. "My mother taught me to do this."

She took a tuft of Barney's fur, rolled it round her paw, then tied it up with string.

"It's all got to be done like this," she said. "You do that side and I'll do this one."

"Is it going to take long?" sighed Barney. "It's very boring standing still."

"Not half so boring as rolling up your fur," muttered Roger.

"Sssh," said Cornelia. "He's going to look *beautiful*. You dry him off with the hairdryer and then I'll comb him out."

One by one, Cornelia unwound all the
coils and brushed each one round her paw
again. Barney tried not to fidget but he was
so tired of standing still and in any case,

14

he was curious to see how he looked.

"What do you think, Roger?" he said.

"Well," said Roger tactfully, "you certainly look different."

"Come and see," said Cornelia.

Barney stared at his reflection in the mirror, blinked and stared again.

"Cornelia!" he cried. "How could you? You've given me *ringlets*! How can I meet the photographer looking like this? He'll think he's come to the wrong house." He shook himself hard but it was no good. The little ringlets jumped and jiggled with him.

"Don't panic, old chap," said Roger comfortingly. "Cornelia will come up with another idea."

"I don't trust Cornelia," muttered Barney.

"Let's look in my magazine," said Cornelia, "maybe there's something there."

Barney flicked through the pages.

"What about that one?" he said, looking at a picture of the winner of a dog show. His fur had been brushed to a fine shine and

he was wearing a collar of plaited ribbon.

"I'd like to look like that," said Barney.

Cornelia was looking distractedly in her bag for some pins.

"Spread out the page, then, Barney, and I'll do my best to copy it."

"Let *me* see," said Roger. He jumped up onto the table and fell on the hairdryer, blowing Cornelia's hat to the floor. The pages of the magazine fluttered and turned, but Roger didn't notice as he leaped onto the page and studied the photographs.

"Barney," said Roger, "are you sure this is the style you want?"

"Quite sure," said Barney firmly.

Cornelia studied the picture and sighed. "I'll do my best, Barney," she said. "Find me some hair gel, Roger."

First Cornelia combed Barney's fur and then she parted it into sections; from left to right, back to front, top to bottom, along each side and in a spiral down each leg.

Then Roger followed with the gel, patting and pulling and twisting Barney's fur into intricate patterns.

"I didn't think you'd have to do all this," said Barney, hidden behind a curtain of fur. "It looked so simple."

"It may look simple to you," said Cornelia, "but these new styles are very complicated to do."

"Well, you know best, I suppose," said Barney, stifling a squeak as his fur was pulled yet again. He was getting impatient.

20

"Finished!" announced Cornelia.

She led him over to the mirror.

Both Cornelia and Roger jumped as Barney let out a terrific howl.

"Owww! What have you done? You said you'd do it like the dog in the picture."

"But I did, Barney," said Cornelia.

"Here's the picture you chose," said Roger.

Barney stared in horror at the pop star with an extraordinary Punk hair style.

"But – " he howled, "I wanted to look like this dog!"

He turned the pages back to the article on the dog show and showed it to Cornelia.

"What am I going to do?"

But it was too late. There was a ring at the front door.

"The photographer!" they all cried.

"I'll explain," said Cornelia. "I'll tell him to come back tomorrow."

She went to open the door and Barney retreated behind the kitchen cabinet.

"Is this Barney's residence?" asked the photographer.

"It is, but he's not here," said Cornelia.

"That's odd; I've an appointment to see him," said the photographer.

"There's been a mistake," said Cornelia desperately. "He's not available at present."

"Shy, is he?" said the photographer sympathetically. "Funny, isn't it, how some celebrities are so bashful. But I'm sure he'll relax once we get talking. Where shall I start?" And with that, he strode into the living room.

"It's no good," whispered Roger. "You'd better go out and get it over with."

Gingerly, Barney edged through the kitchen door.

He was about to start apologizing when the photographer saw him.

There was a gasp. Then — "Fantastic!" the photographer shouted. "Smile please! Let's have your profile."

And he started to photograph Barney from every angle – looking fierce, looking coy, looking domestic, looking romantic. By the time the photographer had finished, Barney felt quite giddy.

"Well, that's that," said Barney when the photographer had finally left. "There's just one more thing to do, Cornelia."

"What's that?" she said.

"Could you make me look like me again?"

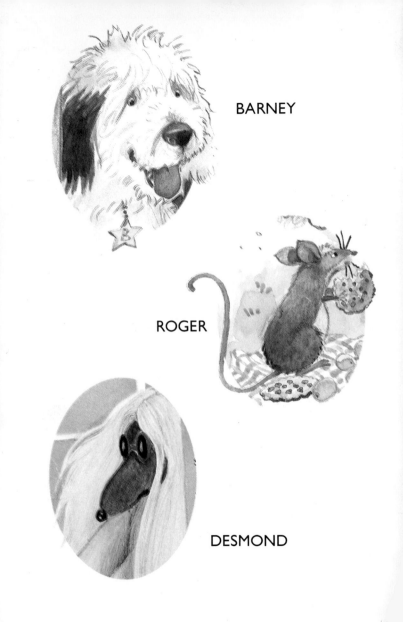

BARNEY

ROGER

DESMOND